# Fish On!

LUCKY LUKE'S
HUNTING
ADVENTURES

Softcover ISBN 13: 978-0-9857179-4-0
Hardcover ISBN 13: 978-1-7327646-4-4


Printed in the United States of America


Cover and interior design by James Monroe Design, LLC.


Lucky Luke, LLC.
4335 Matthew Court
Eagan, Minnesota 55123

**www.KevinLovegreen.com**

Quantity discounts available!

# Chapter 1

I was startled to attention when the line on my twenty-foot fishing rod jerked and the rod was bent toward the pure blue water of the ocean. "FISH ON!" I yelled to the captain. The others with me on the Pirate Ship cheered as the drag from my pure gold reel screamed. The line was zipping out as easy as water flows from a hose. With my eyes bursting and a huge smile on my face, I looked to my right and now I was sitting in a small wooden boat much too small for the ocean.

"Bring him in!" my cousin Tom said, and with a huge tug of my giant fishing rod I felt the enormous weight of the fish at the other end.

"This could be the one, don't lose him!" A voice called out from behind me. I looked over my shoulder and saw my grandpa cheering me on. Bearing down and with superhero strength, I pulled the fish straight up out of the water. The four-hundred-pound bass flew over our heads and landed right in the back of the boat. I jumped up, raising my arms in victory, and then my entire body twitched and woke me up. The image faded quickly in my mind as I realized my face was buried deep in my soft pillow.

A small smile grew on my face as I realized I had just caught the biggest bass in the world, at least in my dreams, but in the real world it was my family's first morning at my favorite place in the world: the cabin. We showed up late last night after the long drive from the city. It's a drive I am used to, since we have been making it since I was born. I didn't even have time to get my fishing stuff unpacked and sorted before my brother Vernon and my sister Crystal and I were directed off to bed by Mom.

Vernon is three years older than me, and he loves to catch fish just about as much as I do. The one thing Vernon doesn't like to do, though, is get up early. That means in the morning, the lake is all mine.

Crystal's only a year and a half older than me, but that still makes me the youngest. She likes to go fishing, but she only goes when Dad takes her out. I think Dad is too easy on her. He puts her bait on, takes her fish off and treats her, well, like a girl. I gave Dad a hard time about it once and he told me, "It's a Dad thing. Maybe one day you'll understand."

There are so many cool things that make my grandpa and grandma's cabin the best place to be. There's the lake itself, of course. But there are also the endless woods, which has been the stage for many thrilling spy adventures and some pretty intense war games for my brother and sister and me. Over the years, we've built the most amazing forts. One time we even tried spending the night in one. If it weren't for the pesky mosquitoes, we would have made it. But instead we were chased back into the cabin, even before our parents had gone to bed.

When we aren't having some kind of adventure around the cabin, the only other place you will find me is down at the lake. I have never seen a lake as amazing as Bapoe's Lake. It was named after my great grandpa, who I don't remember because I was only two when he died. But I keep hearing how I am just like him: a fishing fanatic.

The water in the lake is crystal clear and there are so many fish in it, I believe if the water dried up, you would see fish stacked twenty feet deep. My grandparents' cabin is one of only four cabins on the lake, and in all the years I have been fishing Bapoe's Lake, I have only seen one other boat on it.

After I woke up and realized there was no Pirate Ship, no four-hundred-pound bass, I wanted to see if the sun was up, so I peeked out the window over my brother, who was tucked deep in his sleeping bag, on the little couch next to me. "Yes!" I whispered, not wanting to wake Vernon up. I slid out of my bag and grabbed my jeans, shirt and socks, which were piled up on the floor next to my bed. I quietly walked across the cold, hard floor heading to the porch.

"Good morning." With my eyes still scrunched together as I tried to fully wake up, I greeted Grandpa, who was sitting in his usual rocking chair with a mug of coffee steaming next to him.

"Morning, Luke," he said with a smile. "You're up early as usual. Couldn't you sleep?"

"Nope. I woke up to this awesome dream, where I think I caught the biggest bass in the world."

"Mmmm, sounds like fun," Grandpa said as he took a careful sip of his coffee.

I looked out the windows of the porch to make sure that everything was just the way I remembered it. Like I was looking at a picture, there was the magical lake, as flat as glass with steam floating over the surface. The trees on the other side of the lake were just as clear in the water as they were in the sky.

The dock looked rather peaceful as it lay in the water and Grandpas old pontoon was tucked up on the shore not to far from it. The only thing missing was my little boat, and that would be down there soon.

After focusing on the lake, where I really wanted to be, I scanned the hill to see if there were any animals.

"Any visitors this morning?" I asked.

"Those two big grey squirrels over there and the typical birds at the feeder. That's been it so far."

"Hmm. I'm going to grab a bowl of cereal and get my boat in the water."

"I bet you are. It should be a good morning. The water has been warming up, and the fish should be active," Grandpa said.

I made my way to the kitchen and found the box of Cheerios. I opened the fridge and it was packed so full, I couldn't believe nothing fell out. I grabbed the milk, poured it over my cereal, and headed back out on the porch to sit with Grandpa.

"Well, what are you going to try this morning?" Grandpa asked.

"I think I'll start with my lucky silver Rapala. And if the weeds are too thick I will try a spinnerbait. Do you think those would be good choices to start with?"

"Sounds good to me. Don't forget about the red and white Basserino that I gave you for your twelfth birthday last year. That always seems to work on big bass."

I lifted my bowl and slurped down the last drop of tasty milk, and then I was ready to head out.

"Wish me luck grandpa; off I go to get the big one." I said with excitement.

"Good luck, Luke, but more luck is the last thing you need. You usually have enough luck for the both of us." Grandpa joked.

# Chapter 2

I quietly slid out the front door, making sure not to wake anyone else. I loved to get up early and take advantage of a new day. Grandma always said, "The sun rises each day giving you a chance to enjoy its glory. It's up to you to make the most of it."

What that meant to me was that I had to get outside and have some fun!

As I walked down the top two wooden steps and jumped over the last two, I felt the slight cool of the morning air and couldn't help but smile. The smell of fresh pine and the anticipation of catching fish sent electricity through my body. I was fired up and I loved being up here.

I walked to the side of the garage were my dad's little aluminum boat was leaned up against the wall. I keep telling Dad that he might as well call it my boat, since I am the only one who uses it. He tells me that it was his first boat, and that he bought it with his own money, and that he isn't ready to give it up yet. But I am always welcome to use it. That works for me. I am just glad to have something to fish in.

I just about did a back flip as I tipped the boat over and a rabbit, who must have thought it was a good place to hide, burst out and flashed away. "Whoa, that got me!" I said out loud, as if someone were there with me. I peeked in the window to see if Grandpa had seen me jump. He was still sitting in his chair facing the lake. At least that saved me from some teasing later. I used an old red and white nylon rope I tied to the bow last year to drag the boat around to the front of the garage.

The door was shut to keep out the night critters, like raccoons and skunks. Even though the door appeared to be shut tight, I still opened the door, reached in without stepping into the garage, flipped the light on, and waited for a second or two to listen for scurrying. The coast seemed clear, so I ventured in slowly. I've been greeted unexpectedly by more than one critter in the garage before. We are way back in the woods, so that is to be expected. But it still can be pretty startling.

I opened the big garage door to let more light in and started to gather up my gear. Before I knew it I had the boat loaded with my tackle box, rod, oars, seat cushion, old net, and life jacket. I was ready to start the big pull down to the lake. I grabbed hold of the nylon rope and put all my strength into it. The first few feet were hard, but then I got some momentum going and the boat was moving along pretty well. When I started down the big hill, the boat began to slide faster and faster and before I knew it I was running. I hit the brakes at the bottom and the boat came to a stop.

I took a few deep breaths and then quietly tiptoed onto the dock to see if any fish were hanging around. The crystal-clear water in Bapoe's Lake makes it easy to see fish, but it also makes it easy for them to see you. I walked very slow and peeked over the side and there was the typical assortment of sunfish and a perch or two. I made my way to the end of the long wooden dock and suddenly, out shot a nice largemouth bass. I am good at picking bass out because our lake has a lot of them. They almost look see-through and they have stripes on their sides. This one seemed to be about two pounds, a nice bass. After watching him swim away, I made my way back to the boat and was excited to finally get it in the water.

# Chapter 3

I put my life jacket on and got behind the boat. I bent over and pushed with all my might, shoving the boat into the water. The waves from the boat entering the water broke the perfect glass image of the surface. I watched the little waves, one after the other, roll out into the small lake as if they were on their own journey.

I steadied the boat and eased into the middle seat. With a couple of pulls from the oars I was out far enough to take my first cast. I already had my lucky silver Rapala tied on from the last trip. Pointing my fishing rod in the direction I saw the bass swim, I prepared to make my first mighty cast. I put the line under my right pointer finger, opened the bail of my reel and flung the lure high in the air. It was a long cast and I was proud of myself. I was kind of hoping Grandpa was still sitting up in the window, so he could see how far it went.

I started slowly reeling in the lure, trying to make it look like a real minnow. I didn't get three or four cranks on my reel when the water exploded and my line got tight. It caught me off guard, since this was my first cast! I pulled hard to set the hook and the bass jumped out of the water a full two feet. "YES!" I grunted as I cranked and pulled the bass in. When I had him next to the boat, I reached a hand over the side of the boat and stuck my thumb in his mouth. I

was careful not to get too close to the hooks of my lure. After my dad showed me how to handle a largemouth bass, I am pretty good at getting them in the boat without much of a fight. I learned that bass don't have sharp teeth and it's easy to pick them up if you put your thumb in their mouth and curl up your pointer finger under the bottom lip. You do have to hold on tight, because they usually wiggle once or twice, but then they calm down.

I pulled this beauty out of the water and held it high over my head for Grandpa to see. "Whoohoo!" I half-yelled before I stopped myself quickly, realizing I didn't want to scare the other fish. I get so excited when I catch fish that it's hard for me to stay quiet.

After carefully pulling the hooks out of his mouth, I set him down in the bottom of the boat so I could find my yellow rope stringer. I probably should have been ready with the stringer because by the time I found it in my tackle box, he was flopping around the boat making all kinds of noise. I had to wrestle with him for a while, trying to get another grip on his mouth. I finally pinned him against the side of the boat and got him on the stringer. I flopped him over the edge and back into the water. I tied the stringer up snug so he wouldn't get away and then anxiously grabbed for my rod, ready to make another cast.

I was on my way to catching enough fish for breakfast and I couldn't wait to get another one. I flung that lure high and long several more times but my luck was not as good as that first cast. I wasn't worried, though, because there was a lot of lake left to cover and I was determined to catch more fish.

I set my rod down, picked up the oars, and pulled my way through the water. I knew right where I was heading. I had my plan all mapped out in my head. I had four hot spots that always seemed to hold fish, and I was going to hit each one as I worked my way around the lake.

The first hot spot was just down from the dock a little ways. It was a great spot where the weeds are really thick and the bass love to hide in them. I have to be careful not to cast my Rapala in too far because it will get all tangled in the weeds. The strategy with my floating Rapala is to cast it right next to the weeds and slowly reel it in. The bass usually see it and rush out from in the weeds and inhale it. That's what I was hoping for today, anyway.

I finally made my way to the spot and was careful not to get too close and spook the fish. I positioned myself just right so I could make the first cast count. After taking careful aim, I flung the lure toward the weeds and quickly closed the bail when I realized it was going too far. The lure stopped dead in the air and dropped to the water with a splash, one foot from the weed edge. I smiled. "Yes!" It was a perfect cast, and I knew I had a great chance at getting a bass to strike.

I slowly started to crank and gave the rod tip a little jig to create more action with the lure. BOOM! The water exploded in a blast of spray! I reacted quickly and set the hook with a mighty jerk. Gotcha! "Yes! Yes! Yes!" I clenched my teeth and grunted as I pulled and fought him. This was a nice fish, probably two and a half pounds. He did not want to give in. After two or three big jumps and a couple of powerful deep runs, I reeled him to the side of the boat. With one hand

on my fishing rod, holding it up and away
from the fish, I reached with my left hand
and grabbed my trophy.

After popping the hooks out, I held him up to the sunlight so I could get a good look at him. Actually, it was probably a her. Dad told me that most of the big fish are the females, and we needed them to keep producing more fish for us to catch in the future. So after sizing her up, I decided to ease her back into the cool water. As soon as I let her go, she kicked her tail, splashed me in the face and darted out of sight. Feeling good about letting her go and eager for another fish, I grabbed my fishing rod. I quickly scanned for the edge of the weed bed and launched another cast.

This time I could see the silver flash of my Rapala wiggling just below the surface as two small perch darted back and forth, taking small pecks at it. I don't know what they were thinking, because they weren't much bigger than my lure. "Ha!" I laughed.

"Good luck, little guys. Try picking on someone your own size," I joked.

Pretending I was a pro in a big tournament, I prepared for another cast. When I landed my lure in a little open pocket between the weeds, I smiled. "There's gotta be one there!" I let the lure sit for a second or two and then gave it a couple twitches. BOOM! The water swirled like a tiny tornado and I jerked back hard. To my surprise, there wasn't any tension on the other end and my lure shot out of the water like a rocket over my head. I ducked quickly and smacked my leg with my hand, frustrated at missing a good opportunity.

Quickly reeling in the slack, I tried to hit the same spot. When a hungry bass wants to eat, I've had them hit my lure two or three times in a row. I missed the spot and ended up in the weeds a couple feet deeper in. That was going to be problem, as this was not a weedless lure. I started cranking in line and realized I had the biggest weed bass of the day. I towed the clump of weeds like a sunken ship back to the boat. One long slimy strand at a time, I carefully pulled the weeds free from my lure's hooks. With one smack of the lure on the surface of the water to get the last couple green specks off, I was back in the game.

Given all the action, I figured I had messed up this spot for a while, so I set my rod down and pulled a few strokes with the oars. I carefully scanned the weedline looking for the next dropoff or dark pocket. I didn't go far before seeing weeds coming from the dark water. They looked like long thin snakes swimming for the surface. I knew this spot well and have pulled a bunch of fish out of that dark water.

I quietly eased the oars back in the boat and picked up my rod. Knowing the dropoff goes for a long ways, I reared back and launched my lure as far as I could. I watched as it darted through the air like a little missile. It was a nice cast and I felt like I had a great chance at another fish. I started reeling in the line and quickly felt some hits. I jerked the rod, but nothing was there. I felt them again and jerked again, nothing! When the lure got close enough for me to see, I could tell it wasn't swimming right. There were some long weeds dragging behind, snagged on my hooks. "Those weren't bites, it's time to go weedless," I said to myself.

# Chapter 4

I opened my bail to release my line and quickly went to work. I pulled the weeds off, and a couple bites from my side teeth easily broke the eight-pound-test line. I opened my little green tackle box and flung the Rapala back into the empty slot where it belonged. Pulling the top drawer up and back let me see the second drawer and the bottom of the box. I stared at my two spinnerbaits lying on the bottom, trying to decide which one felt right. I decided to go with the bright green one since it worked the best last time I was out. I grabbed my lucky black rubber worm and shut my box.

I went to work tying a fisherman's knot just like my dad taught me. I ran the loose end of the line through the spinnerbait's eyelet and pulled about ten inches of line to work with. With my left hand I pinched the line and left a gap by the eyelet. With my right hand, I wrapped the loose end of the line five times around the main line going to the reel. I then passed the loose end through the loop next to the eyelet. To get the knot to snug together nice and smooth, I used a little spit. Then I pulled tight and trimmed the loose end with my teeth. "Voila!" I was ready to fish. It took me a long time to get the hang of that knot, but now I can change my lures in no time at all. Adding the finishing touch, so the fish can't resist, I slid my black rubber worm on the hook and made sure it pointed straight out the back.

I sat in the boat, ready for action. Like a machine, I held my line, opened the bail, cocked the rod back, and let her fly. The spinnerbait skirt causes more wind resistance so I can't cast it as far as my Rapala. I put everything I had into it and managed to get it out a good distance into the lake. With a soft splash it plopped into the water and I counted to four one thousand to let it sink. I began reeling fast, because a spinnerbait is supposed to excite a fish into biting. I could feel it bouncing off the long weeds as I raced it in. Nothing. That was ok, because I had faith in this baby. I aimed for a spot ten feet to the left of my first cast. Just like I was standing in the middle of a sliced pizza, I planned to work my way around and cover a large area.

I was cranking in the spinnerbait on my second cast when bam! A giant fish attacked and I responded with a quick and powerful hook set. Pulling hard, the fight was on. I was clenching my teeth and bearing down as my drag started screaming out. This got my heart pumping fast, as most bass aren't big and strong enough to take my drag out. I stopped reeling as the fish took line and just held on. As soon as the drag stopped I started to crank and gain some line back, but it wasn't easy. This was a monster! I started coaching myself to make sure I was doing everything right. I sure didn't want to lose such a beauty. Each time he pulled hard I let up from cranking, but never gave him any slack. That hook wasn't coming out if I could help it.

When I had that monster where I could just about see him, he pulled hard and shot out of the water. Like it was in slow motion, I could see his huge head shaking back and forth and the water drops raining off his body.

*31*

As I watched wide-eyed, my spinnerbait flew out of his mouth and plopped back to the water. In a flash it was quiet, and I was in stunned disbelief. The only proof that something had just happened were the ripples left on the water and the image burned in my memory. I quickly turned and looked at the dock, hoping someone was magically there to witness what had just happened. No one was there. I scanned the lake for anyone else, but the only witness was an eagle perched on a big pine tree a hundred yards away. "Did you see that?" I yelled to the bird. He didn't respond.

I reeled in my line and carefully examined it to make sure it didn't have any wear marks. That was, without a doubt, the biggest bass I had ever seen. I figured it must have weighed five or six pounds.

"Man, that was awesome!" I said with excitement and some disbelief. "Let's do that again."

I cast my spinnerbait in the same spot, hoping the bass was hungry enough to bite a second time. After letting it sink and cranking it in the exact way I did when I hooked the monster, I was bummed out when I didn't get a bite. I tried several more casts, but didn't have any luck. It was time to move on.

I set my rod down carefully and lowered the oars back in to the water. Not wanting to spook the fish, I crouched my head down and eased along, like a ninja oarsman. As I glided, fish were swimming just below the boat and had no worries that I was there. I picked up the oars and let my momentum take me to the next weed bed. I peeked over the side and kept close watch for big bass.

"Whoa," I said under my breath. Sitting next to a big clump of weeds, which looked kind of like a giant hairy mushroom, were two of the biggest crappies I had ever seen. I knew they were crappies because of their flat shape and black speckled sides.

Figuring the crappies were too small to bite my spinnerbait, I quickly went to work. Like a combat surgeon working in the field, I bit my line, opened my box, slipped the spinnerbait in, grabbed a small white jig with a Mr. Twister tail, threaded the line and tied a perfect knot. In record time I was ready to make my cast.

I had glided a little past were I had seen the fish, and I figured my position was perfect for a sneak attack. With a careful and precise cast, I hit the spot a few feet behind the fish. I let my small jig torpedo down through the water, hoping the fish would react to the falling food. I watched the loose line floating on the water. I knew when the line stopped moving down, either the jig had hit the bottom or a fish had taken the bait.

In an instant, my line floating on the water stopped moving. Surprised, but ready for action, I reeled in the slack and gave a steady tug. When I felt the unmistakable twitching at the end of my rod, I was careful, since I had pulled the hook out of more than one soft-mouthed crappie. But when I did set the hook, the fight was good! He did his best to spin around and try to get away. I eased him up to the boat and his silver body shined through the sparkling clear water. I reached for my net and carefully scooped my trophy up.

I laid the net on the bottom of the boat and steadied the fish with my left hand. With my right hand I popped the little hook out of his lip.

As if he knew he was free, he instantly started to flop around like crazy, slapping his body on the bottom of the aluminum boat. He was really kicking up a racket! Not wanting him to spook the other fish, I desperately tried to stop him. I finally smothered him with both hands pinning him to the bottom of the boat. I slid my right hand over the top of his head and back, flattening his spiny fin, and squeezed a firm grip on each side. I picked him up and took a good look at the beauty. This was a very nice crappie; probably one of the biggest I had ever caught. I figured he must be around thirteen or fourteen inches—and that's a nice crappie! With my left hand, I un-tied my stringer and slid the crappie down the line until he met up with the bass.

After snugging up the stringer, I looked up and tried to get my bearings back. With a careful eye, I scanned the surface of the water trying to locate the weed clump. "Good, I didn't go far," I said to myself after pinpointing the spot. There wasn't a hint of wind, so my boat was dead in the water unless I used the oars.

I picked up my trusty fishing rod and lined up another cast. I landed my jig right on top of the weed clump and let it drop. To my total disbelief, in an instant, the line stopped and started twitching. I pulled quick and once again had another brawler at the other end. With an uncontrolled smile on my face, I brought this fish carefully up to the boat and scooped it in. It was another huge crappie! "Yes!" I burst out as I held him out and admired him.

I quickly slid him on the stringer. When I held the stringer high out of the water and analyzed my catch, I felt a rush of pride. I had three perfect fish for breakfast. This was turning into one of the best fishing mornings I had ever had. If I could get a couple more fish on the stringer, I would have enough for everyone for breakfast. My mission was set, and I was determined to catch more.

I flung that little jig around several more times but could not catch another crappie. I did manage to hook two or three little sunfish and while they were fun to catch, they were too small to eat. It was time to try something different.

# Chapter 5

I opened my tackle box and carefully scanned each compartment. When I saw my big red and white Basserino I got a smirk on my face. That's the one, I thought. This baby has caught its share of bass and northern pike. It was one of my favorite birthday presents last year. It's made of soft wood, so it already had cool tooth marks in it from some hungry northern pike. At four inches long and an inch in diameter, it's a big gnarly lure. The water has to be warm and the fish hungry for this guy to work.

I was careful to make sure my knot was tight and strong. I didn't want to lose this baby. I was ready for action, so I rowed my way out to another hot spot. Right smack in the middle of the lake was a deep hole that had those magical long weeds reaching up from the dark water. I wasn't sure if even Grandpa knew about this spot. I found it last year when I was drifting across the lake as I tied on a new lure. When I looked up, I was in the middle of the lake and decided, just for the fun of it, to make a cast. To my surprise, I didn't catch just one fish; I caught three bass bang-bang-bang. I couldn't believe how lucky I was to find this spot.

I eased the boat out, being careful not to get too close. I arched back my fishing rod and shot the lure through the air. Like a rocket, it flew a mile! After hitting the water with a splash, I began reeling it in. I usually reel the Basserino at medium speed to get the right action. It floats when I stop reeling and only goes a couple feet down when I pull it in. When I didn't get a bite on the first two casts, it dawned on me that it might not be going down deep enough for this spot. But I wasn't ready to give up on my lucky lure just yet. My dad always told me, "Persistence and patience pays off in fishing, hunting, and life."

After a bunch of casts, in the middle of a retrieve, my Basserino got nailed! The bite came so hard and fast it caught me off guard, so I was a little late on the set. Before I started reeling, the tension was gone and the fish was off. "Darn!" I blurted. The word didn't get out of my mouth and I felt another tug. I pulled back quickly and like magic I had that fish again. "You really wanted it, didn't you?" I grunted. This guy put up a great fight. He jumped out of the water twice and dove for the bottom several times. In the end, I was the winner. I reached down into the water and hauled in another nice bass. This one I figured to be about two pounds, another perfect eater. Pinching his lip tight with my left hand, I worked the stringer loose with my right and slid him down the line. I admired my stringer for a second and then tied it up snug and was ready to get back at it.

I rifled my lure through the air, again covering a lot of water. I reeled it up, loaded the line and sent it hurling through the air again. I was working the area like a pro, covering every inch of water. On one of my many retrieves I felt a slight tug and yanked hard to set the hook, but nothing was there. Panic flooded my body as I reeled in my line with no tension at all. "No, no, no." I said quietly as I lifted the empty, dangling end of line out of the water. I sat in disbelief staring at the loose line hanging from my fishing rod. What had just happened? I lost my lucky lure? On what? As the thoughts raced through my head, a two-or three-pound northern pike shot out of the water high into the air. My eyes just about popped out of my head when I caught sight of my red and white Basserino dangling from its mouth.

"Did that just happen?" I asked myself. "Are you kidding me?"

That pike's sharp teeth must have hit my line when he bit. Now my lure was stuck in his mouth, gone. I couldn't believe I had just lost one of my favorite lures. Even more, I couldn't believe I had just seen a fish jump with it in its mouth. "Grandpa is never going to believe this!"

Now I had to decide: should I call it a day and head in, or should I tie on another lure and keep fishing? My goal was to catch enough fish to feed everyone for breakfast, and my goal wasn't complete. I dug in my tackle box and pulled out my spinnerbait. In a flash, I was back in the game and ready to go.

I launched a cast out to the middle and counted to four one thousand to let it sink. I raced it back to the boat, hoping for some action. On my third cast it got attacked, and I reacted faster than a horse kick. I fought that beauty for at least two minutes. It even pulled out drag a couple of times. In the end, I again was the victor. I pulled that bass out of the water and held her up high, like a real trophy. I pulled my hook out, kissed the top of the bass's head and slid it back in the water. I had to laugh at myself. I had seen a pro fisherman do that during a bass tournament on TV, and I had to give it a try.

There was no surprise; it was as slimy as I thought it would be.

Just when I was ready to make another cast, something caught my eye off to my left. It couldn't be! There floating on the surface about twenty yards away was my Basserino! "Sweet!" I quickly set my rod down and rowed over to it. I was so excited to get my lucky lure back. When I got about a boat length away, I saw a swirl and a splash and my lure disappeared. I looked down in the water and could see the northern pike swimming away slowly with my lure hooked in the side of its mouth. "Whoa." That was one of the coolest things I had ever seen. Then it hit me, there goes my lure again! Just when I thought it was going to be my lucky day, my luck ran out. As the fish disappeared into the dark of the deep water, I decided to get back to fishing.

I grabbed my rod and launched a nice cast across to the weeds. I started reeling and instantly my spinnerbait was hit. "Boom!" I said as I pulled hard. It was another great bass. What a day this was turning out to be! I enjoyed every minute of the fight this guy had for me. I pulled him in and decided he was a perfect eater, so I slid him on my amazing stringer of fish. It now held three bass and two crappies, enough for a wonderful breakfast for everyone. I tied the stringer extra tight and plopped the fish back in the water.

I looked up, ready to make another cast, and to my absolute amazement, there was my Basserino floating on the surface again. "You have got to be kidding me." I said, shaking my head. I figured I had to try again. Easing the oars into the water, I pushed my way closer to the lure. Just like before, about a boat length away, swirl, splash, and it was gone. Once again, the hope of getting my lucky lure back faded.

It was clear that this was turning into one of the best fishing adventures I'd ever had. "Let's see what happens next," I said as I flung my spinnerbait high in the air for another chance at a fish. Just as I retrieved my spinnerbait within sight of the boat, a fish shot in and attacked it. Reacting was easy, because if I didn't react fast, my rod was going to be swimming with the fish. I pulled and held my rod high, and the fish ran like it was being electrocuted. I quickly realized this was not another bass. This must be a small, rowdy, northern pike. When I got him close, he exploded out of the water and did a tail-walk the whole length of the boat. "Impressive, little guy!" I said to him. I finally scooped him up in the net, but the game wasn't over. Either he didn't like being hooked, being in the net, being near me, or all of the above. It took me several minutes to get this little dude to calm down so I could get the hook out.

I finally got a grip of that slimy, slippery fish and unhooked him and slid him back into the water. His last attempt to show me his disapproval of the whole ordeal was to whip his tail and fill my face with water. "You little turkey!" I said, shaking the water off of my face. I washed the pike slime off my hands in the fresh water. And while the slime came off easily enough, that smell sure stuck with me. Northern pike have a layer of slime on their body that smells terrible and gets on everything when you haul them into the boat. If you can get past the slime, they are fun to catch and pretty good eating.

# Chapter 6

I scanned the water, looking for my next target and there it was again. My lure, floating on the surface about fifteen yards away. I thought for a minute and decided to try something crazy. The slightest breeze had come up and was easing across the water in the direction of the lure. I gave myself one medium push with the oars and then rested them on the seats of the boat. I picked up my net and dipped it in the water. The boat's momentum was carrying me right to my target. I couldn't believe my plan was working. The wind even turned the boat to the side so the net was now leading the way. It was crunch time, because I was now at that magical boat length away and I was dying to see if the fish would spook or give me a chance.

Suddenly, my lure sank like a submarine below the surface. But it didn't splash away like before. I saw the pike, with my lure hanging from his mouth, about two feet below the surface. In the crystal clear water it seemed like I was looking in a fish tank at the doctor's office. I held perfectly still and, to my utter amazement, the fish stayed in one place and the net slowly swallowed it. "Gotcha!"

With my prize captured, I quickly lifted the net into the boat. The fish must have decided to give up, because he barely even put up a fight. I carefully pulled my hooks out and eased the fish back in to the water.

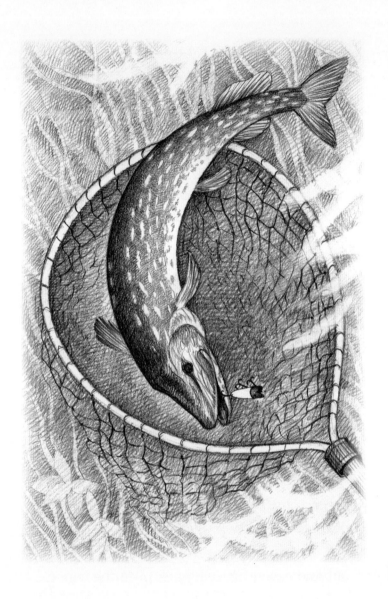

"Thanks buddy, you deserve to go free." I said as he swam off.

"One thing for sure, no one is going to believe that just happened," I said to my re-captured Basserino.

I realized then that my stomach was growling for food and I had plenty of fish and stories from this great morning. Grabbing the oars, I pulled hard and steady and whistled my way back across the lake.

Just as I pulled up to the shore, my buddy Fletcher, our chubby yellow lab, came running down to see what I was up to. "Hi boy, you won't believe what I have to show you." His tail wagged a little faster with curiosity. "Check out these beauties." I held the heavy stringer up high.

I hopped out of the boat, now with the fish slung over my right shoulder and resting on my back. Fletcher, bouncing up and down, kept sticking his nose on the fish to get a good whiff. "What do you think about that, boy? Did I do good today or what? I bet you would like to get hold of one these babies."

Suddenly, Fletcher did just that. He grabbed the lowest-hanging bass and just about pulled me over backwards. "Leave it, leave it, No!" I scolded. He let go and I quickly checked out the fish to make sure it wasn't ruined. "You're lucky, you silly dog. Now leave them alone, they're not for you."

As Fletch and I made our way up the big hill, Mom must have seen us coming. She was already around the side of the cabin with her camera.

"Looks like someone did pretty well this morning!" Mom said.

"You bet I did. It was one of the best days I have ever had on the lake," I piped back.

The back door of the cabin opened and out came Grandma, Grandpa, Dad, Vernon, and Crystal.

"Check it out! Not a bad day on the water," I said as I proudly heaved the stringer out in front of me.

"I've never seen crappies that big come out of this lake!" Grandpa was amazed. "What did you catch them on and where did you get them?"

"A fisherman is never supposed to give up his secrets," I joked with Grandpa.

"Yah, yah." Grandpa spouted back.

"I got them with my little white Mr. Twister. I caught both of them in my first hot spot just down the shore. If you can believe it, I saw them both hanging out next to this big weed clump that looked just like a big hairy mushroom. I did the sneak attack and went back and dropped my jig right on their heads and they both nailed it, one after the other. It was awesome!"

"Good for you Luke! You are quite the fisherman," Grandma said with pride. "The apple sure didn't fall far from the tree."

"What did you catch the bass on?" Vernon asked.

"I think they would have bit on anything today. But I used a Rapala, spinnerbait and my Basserino. And you won't believe what happened to my Basserino. It was almost its last day."

"Sounds like a good story for breakfast. Let your mom take a picture and then you clean those fish up. I'll get back to the kitchen and get the oil hot." Grandma was off.

"Sounds good, I will have a stack of filets inside in no time," I replied.

"You kids all get together, this will be a great picture," Mom said.

Vernon and Crystal moved in for the shot. Crystal did her best not to get any fish slime on her. I held the fish out as high and far as I could to make them look as big as possible. Mom snapped a couple pictures and then Vernon and I each held one end of the stringer and had Crystal stand in the middle for one more shot.

"Here's to a magic day. CHEEEEEEESE!" I said with a giant smile.

# About the author

Kevin Lovegreen was born, raised, and lives in Minnesota with his loving wife and two amazing children. Hunting, fishing, and the outdoors have always been a big part of his life. From chasing squirrels as a child to chasing elk as an adult, Kevin loves the thrill of hunting, but even more, he loves telling the stories of the adventure. Presenting at schools and connecting with kids about the outdoors, is one of his favorite things to do.

Monster Mule Deer

Lucky Luke's
25lb. turkey

The
Muddy
Elk

Crystal
1st buc

Lucky Luke
with a large
mouth bass

Lucky Luke's
1st bear

Crystal, The Swamp hero!

www.KevinLovegreen.com

# Other books in the series

To order books, sign up for book alerts, or to
see great pictures visit:

## www.KevinLovegreen.com

A note to the reader,

All the stories in the Lucky Luke's Hunting Adventures series are based on real experiences that happened to me or my family.

If you like the book, please help spread the word by telling all your friends!

Thanks for reading!
Kevin Lovegreen